THE FEARSOME INN

THE FEARSOME·INN

by Isaac Bashevis Singer

Translated by the author and Elizabeth Shub

Illustrated by Nonny Hogrogian

AN ALADDIN BOOK
Atheneum

Originally published by
CHARLES SCRIBNER'S SONS

Originally published by Charles Scribner's Sons
Text copyright © 1967 Isaac Bashevis Singer
Illustrations copyright © 1967 Nonny Hogrogian
This book published simultaneously in the
United States of America and in Canada
Copyright under the Berne Convention
All rights reserved
No part of this book may be reproduced in any form
without the permission of Charles Scribner's Sons
Printed in the United States of America
Library of Congress Catalog Card Number 67-23693
ISBN 0-689-70769-X
First Aladdin Edition, 1984

THE FEARSOME INN

I<small>T WAS AS IF THE SNOW TREASURES OF HEAVEN HAD BEEN OPENED.</small>
The snow fell day and night, sometimes straight down and sometimes slanting. Now and then it swirled in the air like a dog chasing its tail. All the roads were covered. The branches of the trees, glazed with ice, resembled the arms of crystal candelabras. In the middle of a field stood what was left of a scarecrow. It shook in the wind, flapping its rags and laughing madly.

On a hill overgrown with thistles, by a windmill with a broken vane and a smithy whose forge had long been cold, stood the inn that belonged to Doboshova, the witch. She was the widow of Dobosh, the famous highwayman. For forty years Dobosh had preyed on the roads of Poland, robbing merchants on the way to Warsaw, Cracow, Danzig, Leipzig, and had amassed a huge fortune. When he was finally caught and hanged, Doboshova married Lapitut, her present husband, who was half man, half devil. They settled in the inn and kept themselves busy plying their witchcraft on travelers who stumbled their way.

Doboshova held captive three girls who were her servants. One was called Reitze, one Leitze, and the third Neitze. Reitze had black hair and black eyes, Leitze blonde hair and blue eyes, and Neitze red hair and green eyes. The girls slaved all day long. At night they slept in the hayloft with the rats and field mice. Many times they tried to escape, but Doboshova and Lapitut had cast a spell on the road so that it led nowhere. Each time a girl tried to run away, she wandered around in circles and returned to the inn completely exhausted. When this happened, Doboshova soaked a reed whip in slops to make it supple. Lapitut gave the girl thirty-nine lashes.

In the summertime wayfarers seldom came to the inn. But in the winter, when blizzards wiped out the roads, travelers often lost their way, and victims were plentiful. This particular morning three young men had strayed to the inn. One was called Herschel. He was on his way on foot to the Yeshiva of Lublin and had taken a wrong turn in the storm. The second, Velvel, had been traveling by sleigh to the city of Lemberg to buy merchandise for his father's store. He had fallen asleep and had slipped off the sleigh. The howling wind had prevented the coachmen from hearing him call. Velvel wandered about looking for shelter and finally found himself at Doboshova's inn. The third, Leibel, was returning home from a faraway city where he had been studying the cabala, the ancient Hebrew books that reveal the mysteries of heaven and earth. As a parting gift, his master had given him a piece of chalk, saying, "If you draw a line around man or beast with this piece of chalk, it will imprison them in a circle. Not only will they be unable to escape but no one will be able to get into the magic ring." But the chalk was of no help in a snowstorm, and Leibel, too, arrived at the inn.

When Doboshova and Lapitut saw the three young guests, they were overjoyed. Doboshova looked like any other innkeeper. But like all witches she had an elflock, which she kept well-hidden under a cap. Lapitut had a stumpy horn on his forehead. However, he carefully combed his matted hair down to cover it. The three young men were wet through and frozen. Doboshova led them to the stove so their clothes could dry out and gave orders to the girls to prepare the oven for baking.

"You must be hungry," she said to the young men. "Be kind enough to wait just a bit. I always serve my guests hot rolls fresh from the oven." To Lapitut she said, "Go to the well and fetch water for the barrel so that our visitors can wash their hands and make the benediction before their meal."

The three girls, Reitze, Leitze, and Neitze, knew what was in store for the young men, but they dared not give even a word of warning. First of all, if Lapitut were to catch them, he would whip them to death. Secondly, they knew only too well that all roads led back to the inn.

Everybody went to work at once. Reitze added wood to the oven. Leitze put flour in a bowl and mixed some dough. Neitze kneaded it and shaped it into rolls. Doboshova herself sprinkled the rolls with something that resembled caraway seed. Actually, it was an herb, the very smell of which, when baked, gave nightmares to those Doboshova wanted to ensnare. When the rolls were baked and about to be removed from the oven, Doboshova said to the young men, "You'll find three dippers and three towels by the barrel. Go and wash your hands.

The moment you are ready, the rolls will be taken out, and they will be hot and crisp. You can smell them now."

"You are a good housekeeper," Herschel said.

"I wish I could find a wife like you," added Velvel.

"It brings good luck to treat wayfarers well," stated Leibel, the cabala student.

Each took hold of a dipper and bent over the barrel. In that very instant the spicy smell of the herb-covered rolls took effect. All three young men suddenly felt dizzy and began to dream.

Herschel dreamed that he was a slave in a strange land. He had become a trainer of wild beasts. His master, a prince, had ordered him to teach a huge lion, called Arieh, the most dangerous of tricks. Herschel was to make the lion keep its jaws open while he placed his head in the beast's mouth. Then the animal was to close its jaws just enough so as not to harm Herschel and release him on command. At last the trick was learned, and the day came when Herschel was to perform for the first time before the prince and his court. Herschel was in the lion's cage making one last test before the performance. He placed his head in the lion's mouth, patted him on the neck, and after a minute called, "Arieh, enough!" But Arieh did not loosen his jaws. Herschel patted him again and coaxed, "Arieh, enough! Open your mouth!"

But the lion did not move. Instead he began to roar so terrifyingly that Herschel felt his blood freezing in his veins. The roaring continued, louder and louder, until Herschel could hardly breathe. "God save me," he prayed.

This was Herschel's nightmare.

Velvel also dreamed he was in a strange land. He knew no one. He looked for work but couldn't find any. Finally he had to beg to eat. One late afternoon he found himself on a street with many buildings. He walked through a gate into a courtyard. He turned to leave, but it had become dark, and he couldn't find his way. He called out, but no one heard him. Groping along a wall, he found an opening. He entered it, hoping it would bring him back to the street. Instead a stairway led him downward. It got darker and darker. Suddenly he came to a large room. In the glow of the single oil lamp he saw bricks of solid gold, barrels filled with coins. He had stumbled into the vault of the king's mint.

Velvel knew that if he were discovered he would be taken for a thief. He searched the room for the opening through which he had come. He soon found it, but at that moment two workmen appeared and began to close it up with bricks. He crouched in a corner so they would not see him, yet he knew that he had to get out before their work was finished or he would remain without bread and water, perhaps even without air to breathe.

Did he dare ask the workmen to let him out? They would believe that he was there to steal the gold. They would summon the guards. He would be put in chains and thrown into a dungeon. They might torture him. Finally he decided that it would be better to appeal to the mercy of the workmen than be buried alive with the King's treasure. Just as he stepped from his corner, the last brick moved into place, and the lamp flickered out. "Wait!" he shouted with all his might, but it was too late.

This was Velvel's nightmare.

Leibel dreamed that he was in a desert. He was hungry and thirsty. After long searching, all he found was a dried-out stream, in the middle of which lay snakes, crocodiles, and lizards. They looked as hungry and parched as he. Their mouths were wide open, showing their pointed teeth. The trunk of a tree lay across the bed of the stream. On the other side, Leibel saw a grove of date palms surrounding what looked like a shimmering pool. Leibel realized that one false step could land him among the monsters. But his thirst was so great that he was prepared to take the risk. He stepped onto the tree trunk and spread out his arms to help him keep his balance as he made his way across.

He had reached the middle of the stream when he saw coming toward him a woman whom he recognized immediately as a witch. Her head was covered with elflocks, and she had the webbed feet of a goose. Even though she did not resemble her, somehow she reminded him of Doboshova.

Leibel stopped in his tracks. To fall into the hands of such a creature was even worse than being devoured by crocodiles. He turned carefully back to retrace his steps, only to see a male devil coming toward him. A short horn, which spun like a top, protruded from his forehead. Even though he did not resemble him, somehow he reminded Leibel of Lapitut.

"O Holy Powers, what shall I do now?" cried Leibel in terror.

This was Leibel's nightmare.

At the same moment, all three—Herschel, Velvel and Leibel—awoke. Their nightmares, which had seemed so long, in reality had lasted only a few seconds. All three still stood bent over the barrel as they heard Doboshova saying, "Well, why don't you wash your hands, my dear lads? The girls are taking the rolls out of the oven."

Dazed, all three washed their hands and wiped them. At last they were seated at the table. Herschel and Velvel were about to recite the benediction for bread and begin eating. Had they done this, they would have been lost, because in addition to the diabolic seeds, Doboshova had put a potion into the dough that deprived human beings of all will. But all at once Leibel cried out, "Wait!"

"What's the matter?" asked Herschel.

"Why?" added Velvel.

"Eat, young men," Doboshova urged in a wheedling tone.

"What is this?" Lapitut grumbled.

"While getting the water, I lost my ring in the barrel," Leibel explained quickly. "It was a family heirloom that goes all the way back to King Solomon. It was given to him by the Queen of Sheba. It can show the way to buried riches, locate sunken ships and caravans covered by the sands of the desert. It can also heal the sick and make the old young. I beg of you, help me find my ring."

Despite the many treasures that they already had, the greed of Doboshova and Lapitut could not be satisfied. Even more important, they had a great desire to be young again. When they heard what the ring could do, they both ran to the barrel and stuck their hands into the water to search for it.

Leibel jumped up, rushed over to Doboshova and Lapitut and quickly drew a circle around them with his chalk.

When the two could find no ring in the barrel, they straightened up, ready to return to the table, but they could not step beyond the magic line surrounding them.

"What's going on here?" growled Lapitut.

"What's this circle?" screamed Doboshova.

Reitze, Leitze, and Neitze stood openmouthed.

Herschel and Velvel sat without saying a word, as if they had lost their tongues in astonishment.

This is what had happened.

Just as Leibel was about to say the benediction, he had glanced at Doboshova, and it had suddenly struck him that she resembled the witch he had seen in his nightmare. He cast a quick look at Lapitut and recognized the devil in his dream. Leibel, who had studied the cabala and knew something about the tricks of the Evil Host, realized that there was something wrong here and that he must act immediately. He made up the story about the ring to prevent the boys from eating.

Held within the magic boundary, Doboshova and Lapitut were the captives for the first time in their lives. As soon as Leitze, Reitze, and Neitze were convinced that Doboshova and Lapitut had lost their power, they told the young men about all they had suffered under the wicked couple's spell.

All three had parents, sisters, and brothers who had surely searched for them, but since the road to the inn was bewitched, their relatives had been unable to find them.

As the girls related how they had been tricked away from their homes, Doboshova shouted and waved her fists. She threatened to turn them all into hedgehogs, rats, and skunks. Lapitut shouted that he would whip them to death. But Leibel assured the girls that they no longer had anything to fear. To prevent any devils from coming to the aid of their kin, Leibel made a chalk line along the inside of the entire house and around all the doors and windows. He also circled the oven and the fireplace to make sure that no evil spirit could get in through the chimney.

It soon became clear that all these precautions were needed. No sooner did Doboshova and Lapitut discover they were trapped than they began to call on the dark forces of the forest to come to their rescue. In no time there began to arrive demons, devils, imps, sprites, and other impure spirits. Some appeared as snakes with wings, others as huge bats, and still others looked like rams, weasels, and toads. Had Leibel not protected the house with his magic chalk, they would have swarmed in. Instead they hovered around the windows screeching and threatening those inside.

"There's no reason to fear them," Leibel again reassured the young people. "They can do us no harm. It's time to prepare some food, so that we can eat."

Reitze, Leitze, and Neitze set about making fresh dough without potions and magic caraway seeds. They baked rolls, pretzels, and cookies and made a delicious meal. Reitze was the best baker, Leitze excelled in roasting, and Neitze could fry the crispest food. The good smells filled the house. Doboshova and Lapitut became exceedingly hungry and begged for food. But Leibel said, "We won't give you a bite unless you sign a pledge in your blood that you will leave the inn and return to the Lower Regions."

This Doboshova and Lapitut refused to do. Devils and witches can easily break a promise, but once they have signed in blood they must keep their word or lose their powers forever.

When the evil pair realized that they were getting nowhere with threats, they tried flattery. They called Leibel a master of the cabala. They complimented Herschel and Velvel and even had something nice to say about the girls. They promised all kinds of gifts. Reitze, Leitze, and Neitze were to get beautiful dresses, precious jewelry, and silk underclothing embroidered in gold. Lapitut swore he would teach the young men never-heard-of magic tricks.

"We want neither your gifts nor your teachings," Leibel replied.

For hours Doboshova and Lapitut alternated between curses and coaxing. The devils outside continued their racket, pressing against the windows. Inside, the young people knew that they were safe, protected by the magic chalk.

The winter day passed quickly. Night brought new terrors and temptations. The evil ones laughed and cried, imitated the sounds of trumpets and horns, bleated and hopped about, blasphemed and boasted of their ungodly powers. Some of the creatures of darkness decided to tempt the young people by disguising themselves as beautiful girls, handsome noblemen. The night suddenly became day. The snow outside turned into a sunlit, flower-filled meadow, through which a blue stream flowed. A devil called Topiel, who specialized in luring humans into the water so that they would drown, sang one of his most entrancing melodies to get the young people out of the house. But Leibel would not let any of them succumb, explaining that it was all a delusion.

When the black band saw that no one was coming out, they brought back the night. Three black cats with eyes like green fire appeared in a window. Their meowing was like the ringing of bells.

After a while the cats, too, vanished. Instead a whirling wind shook the roof and whistled in the chimney. There was a howling of wolves and a growling of bears. The outdoors turned fiery red as if reflecting a great conflagration. It began to thunder and lightning, and the inn swayed as in an earthquake. The young people could not help being afraid, but they trusted Leibel and ate their supper while the demons raged.

"No matter how strong the devil is," Leibel said, "God is stronger."

Immediately after supper, the three girls undressed and went to sleep in the same large bed so that they would be less frightened. They put blindfolds on their eyes and cotton in their ears so as not to see the terrifying sights and not to hear the mocking voices of the fiends. Herschel and Velvel made themselves a bed on the top of the large brick oven. They were so exhausted that they soon fell into a deep sleep. Leibel stayed awake to keep watch. He knew that Doboshova and Lapitut could not hold out much longer. He had a parchment scroll and a sharp quill pen in readiness. One by one the monsters outside tired and departed, each for his own lair. Doboshova and Lapitut were left alone. Leibel overheard Doboshova whispering to Lapitut:

"We can't escape. We'll have to sign."

"I wish I'd never known you," Lapitut snarled in reply.

"If you won't sign now," Leibel called out, "I will go to bed, and you'll have to stand on your feet until morning."

"Oh, I cannot stand another minute," Doboshova moaned.

"I'm dying of hunger," Lapitut wailed. "I can't do without a smoke of mandrake root. If only you'd reach me my pipe."

"Sign the oath, and you will have all you need."

The pair had no choice. They each pricked a wrist with the point of the quill and signed their oath in blood:

I, the witch Doboshova, and I, the devil Lapitut, swear by Satan, Lillith, and by all the impure powers to leave this inn, never to return, neither we nor our children, grandchildren, and great grandchildren to the tenth generation. We leave all our possessions to our guests Herschel, Velvel, and Leibel, and to our onetime servants, Reitze, Leitze, and Neitze. Furthermore, the treasure of the late highwayman Dobosh, hidden in the hollow of the old oak in the yard, is from now on also to belong to the aforementioned parties. Furthermore, we remove all spells, charms, witchcraft, evil signs, and curses from the inn and its surroundings and command that everything return to the state it was in before we came. Signed: *Lapitut, the son of Briri, the son of Shabriri, the son of Karteigus, and so on back to my ancestor Satan. Doboshova, the daughter of Naamah, the daughter of Igrath, the daughter of Machlath, and so on back to my grandmother Lillith the First.*

The haggling had continued for so long that the sky was beginning to gray with the light of dawn. The young people had awakened. They watched as Leibel erased a small section of the circle around Doboshova and Lapitut and another bit under a window. Then, opening the window, he called in Aramaic, "*Pik,* out."

Doboshova and Lapitut turned into shadows and vanished. Off they went to the desert of deserts, to the wastes of the netherworld, behind the Mountains of Darkness where there is neither day nor night and dusk is eternal.

The girls were so happy they began to cry for joy.

"Why cry?" Leibel said. "Your troubles are over. The road is open and each of us can return home."

But neither the boys nor the girls made a move to go. The truth is that the inn, which only a few minutes before had looked so gloomy, was now cozy and pleasant. The snow shimmered in the sunlight. Ice spears hung from the roof, reflecting the colors of the rainbow. From the nearby woods came the sound of winter birds chirping and trilling. The smell of pine filled the air.

After breakfast, Leibel led the young people outside to the huge oak tree that was hundreds of years old. There was a great hollow in its trunk. At the back of the hollow they discovered chests full of gold and precious stones. The jewels lit up the darkness. When the girls saw the treasure, they began to scream with delight. But, even with so many riches to take home, not one of them thought of leaving.

The reason was that the greatest magic of all had begun to do its work among them.

Of course, all three girls were filled with admiration and love for Leibel. Had he not driven away Doboshova and Lapitut and the other devils? However, they all knew that Leibel could marry only one of them, and Herschel and Velvel, too, were charming fellows. But who should marry whom?

Again they decided to trust to Leibel's wisdom. And Leibel said, "Let each of us write down on a slip of paper the name of the one we love best and the one we love next best. Then we will study our choices, and we will know what to do."

It turned out that each girl's first choice remained Leibel, but when it came to second choice, Reitze chose Herschel and Leitze chose Velvel but Neitze's second choice was the same as her first. It so happened that Herschel's first choice was Reitze and Velvel's Leitze. As for Leibel, he, too, had made only one choice: Neitze. When the slips were read out, it was quite clear who should marry whom.

At first the girls thought the weddings should be postponed so that they could invite their parents and friends. But all three boys were eager to get married, and Leibel said, "We can arrange the wedding ceremonies right now and later make a big celebration and invite everyone."

Since they had Dobosh's treasure, there was no lack of wedding rings. The girls found a large embroidered shawl that with the aid of four sticks made a perfect bridal canopy. As there were six young people, four of them could hold up the canopy while a pair stood beneath it for the ceremony. The first pair were Herschel and Reitze. They were the oldest. Herschel, the bridegroom, placed the wedding band on Reitze's finger and recited, "With this ring thou art consecrated to me according to the law of Moses and Israel." Bride and bridegroom both sipped wine from the same goblet and the rest called out, *"Mazel tov."* Then in turn the other two couples stood beneath the canopy. And so they were married, according to the strictest law of the Talmud.

The brides had found beautiful dresses in Doboshova's cup-boards, and even though the clothes were long out of fashion, they looked splendid in them. Reitze and Leitze were a little envious of Neitze because she had been chosen by Leibel, but they wished her luck with all their hearts just the same. And although Leibel had studied the cabala and was generally better educated than the others, Herschel and Velvel were both taller and better looking. Besides, Herschel, the Yeshiva student, was a scholar in his own way. As for Velvel, he was an excellent businessman and clever in practical matters. None of the girls had made a bad bargain.

For the time being, all the couples remained at the inn. They sent word to their relatives and friends to tell them they were safe and to invite them to a great wedding celebration. Because some of the guests had to come from distant places, the celebration was postponed until spring.

Now that the inn was no longer spellbound, its entire surroundings had changed. Doboshova and Lapitut had thrown a curse on all the land for miles around. Suddenly streams, hills, and valleys appeared where there had been nothing but flat wasteland. Rabbits, deer, wild ducks, geese, pheasants, and other animals abounded where before there had been no living creatures. Winter passed. Spring came. The sky was blue and clear. The earth was richly covered with grass, flowers, and shrubbery. Trees that had seemed dead bore leaves and blossoms.

Word had spread about the inn that, like a mirage, had for years appeared only to those unlucky enough to go astray.

On the thirty-third day after the first day of Passover the celebration took place. In addition to the guests, people came from all over the country to admire the changed inn and the three happy couples. Wedding jesters and musicians arrived from nearby towns to take part in the festivities. Magicians outdid each other to entertain the crowd with their tricks. After many entreaties, Leibel agreed to show his guests how the magic chalk 'that had saved the young people worked. He fetched the liveliest rooster from the barn, stood him on a table, and drew a circle around him. No matter how strongly the rooster flapped his wings, he could not fly off the table until Leibel wiped away the chalk to free him. Everybody was amazed.

They sang, danced, and made merry for seven days and seven nights. The moon was full and threw a silver light over the entire landscape. Even though there was not room enough in the inn for so many people and many of the guests slept outdoors, no evil intruder dared to disturb or frighten anyone.

After the last guest had left, it was time for Herschel and Velvel to go home with their wives, as had been decided. Leibel and Neitze had made up their minds to remain in the inn. Because, Leibel said, "People often go astray, especially in the winter, and there should be someone to give them food and shelter." Leibel and Neitze were determined never to take any money from their guests, since Dobosh's treasure had made them rich.

The couples said good-bye to each other, and Leibel returned to his studies of the holy cabala, the wisdom of which can never be learned in full.

As the years went by, Herschel completed his education and became the head of a Yeshiva. He used his money to help poor students.

Velvel became a great merchant and was renowned as a man of charity. All three couples lived happily and had many children and grandchildren. It became a custom each year for the couples and their children to gather at the inn and celebrate the day they had been set free.

Since Leibel's ring with the power to make the old young had never existed, Doboshova and Lapitut lived their allotted years and died. However, other devils have taken their place. These still live somewhere far in the desert, in the underground city of Asmodeus their king. It is said that Asmodeus has a beard that reaches to the ground and two huge horns on his head. He sits on a throne held up by four snakes instead of legs. He has many wives, but his favorite is still Lillith, who dances for him each night to the caterwauling of a devil's band.

In time the once fearsome inn became known as the greatest academy of the cabala. It is believed that the ancient cabalists could, with the power of holy words, create pigeons, sap wine from a wall, and take seven-league steps.

In his old age Leibel was no longer called merely Leibel, but the saintly Reb Leib. His beard became white as silver. He could cure the sick with a touch, know what was happening in faraway cities, and foresee the future. Neitze, even though she was busy with her grandchildren — most of whom had red hair and green eyes — helped her husband and copied his writings with a quill pen.

The inn was a haven for all travelers who lost their way. It was said that no candles or oil lamps were needed there at night, because angels, seraphim, and cherubs descended at dark and lit the inn with heavenly light.